TRACTOR

by CRAIG BROWN

GREENWILLOW BOOKS, NEW YORK

The farmer drives the tractor.
The tractor tows
the manure spreader.

Then the tractor tows the plow.

Then the tractor tows the disc.

Then the tractor tows the harrow.

Then the tractor tows the planter.

The seeds sprout.
Some days the sun shines.
Some days it rains.
The plants grow.

Then the tractor
tows the cultivator.
The plants keep growing.

Then it is time.
The tractor tows
the picker and the wagon.

When the wagon is full,
the tractor tows
its load of sweet corn
to a roadside stand.

MANURE SPREADER—Spreads manure on the field before it is plowed, to fertilize the soil. This is the first machine used in the spring.

PLOW—Breaks up the earth into clods and mixes in the manure.

HARROW—Breaks up the clumps of earth into a fine soil, ready for planting.

DISC—Breaks up the clods of earth into smaller clumps.

THE MACHINES

PICKER—Picks the ears of corn off the stalks and drops them in a wagon, leaving the stalks behind.

PLANTER—Drops seeds in rows approximately eight inches apart, then covers them with soil.

CULTIVATOR—Loosens weeds between the crop rows. The cultivator is used three times while the plants are growing, until the plants are too tall for the cultivator to pass above them.

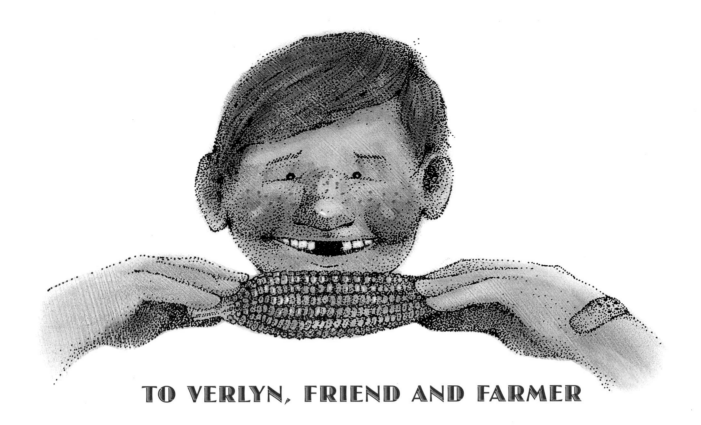

TO VERLYN, FRIEND AND FARMER

Pastels and pen-and-ink were used for the full-color art. The text type is Zapf International.

Greenwillow Books, a division of William Morrow & Company, Inc., 1350 Avenue of the Americas, New York, NY 10019.

Printed in Singapore by Tien Wah Press

First Edition
10 9 8 7 6 5 4 3

Library of Congress Cataloging-in-Publication Data

Brown, Craig McFarland.
Tractor / by Craig Brown.
    p.   cm.
Summary: A farmer uses his tractor to prepare the soil, plant seeds, harvest corn, and haul it away to be sold.
ISBN 0-688-10499-1 (trade).   ISBN 0-688-10500-9 (lib. bdg.)
[1. Tractors—Fiction.   2. Corn—Fiction.   3. Farm life—Fiction.]
I. Title.   PZ7.B81287Tr   1995   [E]—dc20   94-21655   CIP   AC